# SHATTERED HEARTS

A Heartfelt Coming of Age Teen High School Jock Romance Novel

**Disclaimer:**
This is a work of fiction. Names, characters, businesses, places, events, locales, and incidents are either the products of the author's imagination or used in a fictitious manner. Any resemblance to actual persons, living or dead, or actual events is purely coincidental. Author disclaim any liability to any party for any loss, damage, or disruption caused by errors or omissions, whether such errors or omissions result from negligence, accident, or any other cause from this book.

**Copyright:**
In no way is it legal to reproduce, duplicate, or transmit any part of this document in either electronic means or in printed format. Recording of this publication is strictly prohibited and any storage of this document is not allowed unless with written permission from the publisher. All rights reserved.

The information provided herein is stated to be truthful and consistent, in that any liability, in terms of inattention or otherwise, by any usage or abuse of any policies, processes, or directions contained within is the solitary and utter responsibility of the recipient reader. Under no circumstances will any legal responsibility or blame be held against the publisher for any reparation, damages, or monetary loss due to the information herein, either directly or indirectly.

Respective authors own all copyrights not held by the publisher. The information herein is offered for informational purposes solely, and is universal as so. The presentation of the information is without contract or any type of guarantee assurance.

The trademarks that are used are without any consent, and the publication of the trademark is without permission or backing by the trademark owner. All trademarks and brands within this book are for clarifying purposes only and are the owned by the owners themselves, not affiliated with this document

# Table of Contents

| | |
|---|---:|
| CHAPTER 1 | 4 |
| CHAPTER 2 | 11 |
| CHAPTER 3 | 21 |
| CHAPTER 4 | 28 |
| CHAPTER 5 | 35 |
| CHAPTER 6 | 42 |

# CHAPTER 1

It was on the afternoon of the second rain. The bell rang loudly as everyone scattered across the hallway. It was the end of the lectures already. Lizzy packed her books and walked down the hallway with a feeling growing in her, the feeling she could not conclude on. She could sense something bad was about to happen. She walked down to her locker. She opened her locker and threw her books inside and slammed her locker close.

She came face to face with Bryan, her boyfriend, as she closed her locker. She fidgeted and looked scared because she was not expecting to see anyone behind her locker door.

"Scared?" Bryan questioned as he leaned close to the locker.

Lizzy startled, hid behind her books. Bryan looked very tall and handsome on his black jeans and a turtle neck matched with a fitting shoe. He looked very large and his clothes well fitted on him and his eyes piercing.

Lizzy couldn't take her eyes off his well-structured body and his handsome look. She immediately looks away and looks around so that Bryan wouldn't conclude she was thinking about seeing his naked well-structured body like he used to.

Lizzy and Bryan have been dating for almost four years after they met at a friend's birthday party. Lizzy gave Bryan everything. Her body, money, love, and heart that she never thought she could give that much in their relationship. When she met Bryan, she fell head over heels for him and gave him everything just to have him to herself.

"Why did you do that?" She questioned, smiling and acting so shy at her boyfriend's act.

"I'm sorry dear" Bryan answered. He smiled and used his finger to adjust her hair to the back of her ear making Lizzy more beautiful.

"But we need to talk," he said and leaned forward, putting his hands in his jean pocket.

"Oh! Now?" Lizzy asked, giving him a smile. She

stood so calm, patiently waiting for his reply.

"No. Not now" he said.

"I have some things to finish up in class before I involve myself in anything," he explained further.

"You know you can always see me anytime you want to. Just tell me where and when and I will be there' Lizzy said crossly, leaning towards Bryan and acting seductively.

"Can we meet at your place then?" Bryan asked,

looking rather serious.

"Yes, sure," Lizzy said and winked at him with a smile on her face. She leaned toward Bryan to give him a hug.

"I would be at your place by 7 pm." He leaned towards her and gave her a kiss on her forehead not waiting to hear her response. He left almost immediately without looking back at her.

Lizzy turned sharply and glanced at him as he left. She had a mixed feeling about her boyfriend's attitude to her.

"I didn't even remember to ask why he wants to see me, argh!" Lizzy said to herself with disappointment in her voice. She looked confused and walked down to the parking lot.

She got into her white Benz parked alone with no car parked beside hers. She dropped her bag on the seat and turned on the ignition. She accelerated out of the school parking lot and drove down the freeway.

# CHAPTER 2

At 6 pm, Lizzy was on her bed staring at the cracks in the old plaster ceiling of her room. She wore a pair of joggers and a tank top. Her hair was not well done. The door of her room is brown with scratches on the door of her room. Her room is about three lengths of her arm span, including the closet of her room, and a picture of her favorite celebrity on her wall, at the end of her room.

She changed her position looking so disturbed at

what her boyfriend has to say. She stretched her hand to the lower part of her bed in search of her phone. She picked up her phone and checked the time. It was 6:25 pm as at that moment. She stood up from her bed. She went downstairs to the kitchen. She sat at the kitchen counter, and drank water.

She left the kitchen and went to the living room. She sat on the couch expecting her boyfriend to show up at 7 pm as agreed. After a while, she heard the sound of the doorbell. She stood up and adjusted her joggers and her top.

"Hey. Bryan", she said with a smile as she opened the door. She put her arms around him and hugged him hard. He didn't hug her back. She let him go and kissed his lips slowly.

"Come in". She paved the way for him to enter.

"Thank you" Bryan responded and walked into the house. Lizzy shut the door behind her and walked to the living room.

"Can I sit ?" Bryan asked. Lizzy chuckled at his question.

"Yes you can", they both sat down. "Why are you acting like a visitor here? You have been acting strange lately, what's wrong ?" she adjusted her position, now facing Bryan.

"Ermm...I...I..." Bryan tried to find his words. His hands were wet with perspiration as he nervously tried to speak.

"You see Lizzy, I am very sorry. I..." Lizzy cuts him short as he tries to continue with his sentence.

"Why are you sorry? Did you cheat on me ?" Lizzy asked him, now with her hand crossed on her chest, waiting patiently for his answer.

"I didn't cheat on you, babe. I just want my space" He faced her and placed his hands on hers

"Lizzy, you've been an amazing woman so far, and trust me, I enjoyed every bit of us. But it seems I have fallen for another woman. "

"You are in love with another woman? After four years of my life spent with you? Who does that?"

Lizzy said amidst tears in her eyes. She stood up and faced Bryan.

"I think you need to leave now. probably you are drunk." Lizzy said. A tear rolled down her face.

Bryan stood up and adjusted his collar . "Lizzy, I'm not drunk. Breaking up with you is better than cheating on you. And besides, I love her"

Lizzy looked very worried and tears were already coming down her face uncontrollably.

"You are in love with her? How long has this been going on? What did I do to deserve this?" Lizzy grabbed Bryan by his shoulder.

"Please don't go. I love you so much." Lizzy begged.

"But I'm no longer in love with you", he removes her hands from his arm and leaves without another statement.

She fell to her knees and cried profusely. Her thoughts were filled with the memories of herself and Bryan's happy moments together.

"Was this why I was having some weird feelings in the morning? Why is my world crumbling?", she said to herself amidst tears. She grabbed her phone and dialed a number.

"Hey, bitch! What's up? Why do you have to call this late?", the caller said with a loud voice.

"I need you right now. I do need you Pam", she said as tears rolled down her face.

"Babe, what's wrong? You sound like someone's dead. Is grandma dead?

"Bryan broke up with me." Lizzy cried the more as she said those words to Pamela. She ran her hand through her hair and placed her hand on her forehead while she talked to her friend.

"He did what? Why will he do that?" Pamela shouted over the phone surprisingly.

"He's into some woman I don't know"

"We will talk about it in school tomorrow. Please stop crying. You definitely will find a better man than the dick head", Pamela assured her and hung up.

Lizzy lay flat on the floor of the living room with her hands stretched. She cried herself to sleep.

## CHAPTER 3

Lizzy sat at a corner in a club down the street, waiting for Pamela. They had agreed to meet at the club after their lecture in the afternoon. She looked around and didn't see her friend show up. She adjusted her skimpy, armless dress. She let out a sigh of discomfort. The thought of Bryan came to her head.

"No, I can't do this to myself". She took the rest of her drink angrily and wiped her mouth on the back of her hand.

Pamela walked to the club wearing a black fitted blue tank top with a black leather skirt. She looked around for Lizzy and walked up to where she was.

"Babe, are you drunk already?", she sat beside Lizzy and dropped her leather bag on the table.

"No, I'm not. I'm just heartbroken and sad", Lizzy said and gestured at the bartender.

"Please, we need two shots of vodka", Pamela said

to the bartender.

"No, bring a bottle with two glasses", Lizzy requested.

"Don't kill yourself because of a man. He's probably enjoying himself with his new babe", Pamela looked at her friend angrily.

"I saw him in class today. He acted as nothing happened", she wipes her tears. "He's really done with me and I have to move on", she said and smiled at her friend.

The bartender appeared and dropped the bottle of drink on their table. Pamela poured herself and her friend a glass of drink.

"Lizzy, do you know that guy has been checking you out?", she used her face to indicate the direction of the guy. Lizzy looked at the direction to place which guy.

She saw the guy at the bartender's counter. He had blond hair combed neatly and filled beards. He wore jeans, sneakers and a sweatshirt pulled up his arm. He looked at his glass of wine before drinking and looked back at Lizzy.

"He is actually not bad but I'm still not over my ex-boyfriend", she rolled her eyes at Pamela and took the last drink.

"Girl, I need to leave. Grandma wouldn't want me home very late. It's past 11 pm already." Lizzy said looking at her watch.

"I thought we were going to dance and make out with some guys before we leave", Pamela said with a sad expression.

"I'm sorry. Maybe some other time". Lizzy stood up and pulled her friend up. As they were about to leave the club. The guy from the other time walked up to them.

"Excuse me, please," he politely said. Pamela and her friend look back.

"Yes? How can we be of help? Pamela asked.

"I actually want to meet your friend", pointing at

Lizzy.

Lizzy looked surprised, "me?".

"Yes, you. I'm Stan", he responded. "It seems late already, can I take you both home?", Stan looked at them.

"Oh! Of course. But we don't stay together. You can drop her off at her place. I stay three blocks away so I will find my way home." Pamela concluded. She removed her friend's hand from her neck and winked at her friend and left them.

# CHAPTER 4

"Hop in please", Stan opened the Passenger's door.

After the night they met at the club they had already met three other times and gotten so close. Lizzy feels very comfortable having Stan around.

Stan is a businessman. He has two offices and in fact, wants to settle down with any lady ready to love him and settle with him. He walked to the driver's side of the car and opened the door. He sat down and put on his seat belt. He started the car and played music. Lizzy looked at his well-built body. He was wearing a white shirt, with a pin collar black tie with a small gold pattern. His cuff links gleaned in subdued self-satisfaction.

"Where are we headed?", Lizzy asked with her eyes still glued to him.

"Your school of course. Didn't you say you want to pack your books home? He responded.

"oh, yeah. True. Thank you", Lizzy smiled and glued her eyes at cars moving in front

Lizzy finished her final exams last week and Pamela, her friend left for Sweden a week after their final exams leaving Lizzy. Lizzy tried her best to get over her ex-boyfriend by trying to fall in love with Stan

They got to the school's parking lot. Stan pulled into the lot. He faced Lizzy, looking all beautiful on her white crop top and bum short with her hair neatly combed straight back leaning on her shoulders.

"Don't take long", he said to Lizzy. Lizzy nodded her head and stepped out of the car.

After ten minutes, she was carrying a box on her hands filled with books. Stan sighted her from the rearview mirror. He got out of the car and opened the boot.

"Is that all?", he collected the box and dropped it inside the boot.

"Yes", she walked to the car.

They both left the school and Stan went to Lizzy's place to drop her off

In the evening, Lizzy was sitting at the chair in the kitchen glancing through her phone while munching on grapes, her phone rang. It was Pam.

"Hey, Pam! It's been a while", Lizzy said smiling over the phone.

"I know, right? How have you been and how's Stan?", she asked.

"He's just there though", Lizzy squeezed her face and put the phone on her left ear.

"What's wrong, Lizzy? Is he cheating too?", Pam asked surprisingly.

"No. But I don't love him. I think I'm only in love with his looks". She stood up and walked around the kitchen.

"What? Let him know about it then and don't play with his feelings." Pamela advised.

"Okay, I won't. He's taking me to his house tomorrow. Would talk to him about it. I need to go now dear", Lizzy said to Pamela. "Okay, dear. I should give you a call tomorrow.

"Bye", Pamela replied and hung up at her end.

# CHAPTER 5

It was a bright Saturday morning, Stan parked his white Benz in front of Lizzy's house. He waited outside for Lizzy to come out. She opened the front door and walked to Stan smiling.

"You look beautiful", Stan said to her

"Thank you", she replied. They entered the car and left for Stan's house. Stan Parked at his parking lot as he got to his compound. Lizzy got out of the car and looked around surprised.

"Your house is beautiful", she said, still looking surprised. Stan led her inside the house. She said on the couch and got distracted as she was looking around by Stan's voice.

"Do you want some coffee? Juice? Or wine?",Stan offered.

"I'm okay with juice and besides, your house is heart-melting. You stay alone?", she said, still looking around.

"I do. You will meet my brother and parent's soon", he said as he walked to the kitchen to get the juice. He walked back with two glasses of juice.

"Your brother?" She asked.

"Yes, my brother. He finished high school for almost a month now. The funny thing is I don't even know which school", he laughed and sat beside Lizzy.

"That's really bad", she responded and laughed.

He stares at her. She looked at Stan and moved closer to him. She hungrily meets her lips with his and kisses him. She sat up and sat on his lap feeling him on her part. He placed her softly on her back without breaking the kiss. She moved her hands slowly and pulled his clothes off.

His hands found their way towards her shirt. He pulled off her top leaving her with her bra. He kissed her down to her neck and unhook her bra. He placed a soft kiss on her lips and pulled away from her lips. He slightly moved his head to her chest and sucked her chest. She moaned slightly. He tried to put off her shorts when the door opened.

They got scared and quickly made their way to their clothes.

"Stan? What the hell? Why don't you get a room?", the intruder said as he turned his back.

Lizzy dressed and got up to leave, "Maybe we will see some other time", she carries her bag.

"No. Meet my brother first," he looked at his brother. "You can face us dude", he said to his brother.

"Bryan?", Lizzy called his name surprised to see him.

"Do you know him?" Stan asked Lizzy, now facing Bryan.

"What are you doing with my ex-girlfriend Stan?", Bryan asked angrily.

"Bryan is your brother? Lizzy asked with a worried voice. She hissed and left the house.

Stan fell on the couch looking so sad and speechless.

# CHAPTER 6

Few days after the incident occurred, Lizzy decided to move out of the country to start a new life and to find herself. She came out of the washroom all dressed up. She packed her clothes into her box. Stan has been trying to reach her but she turned her phone off.

She went downstairs and sat beside her grandmother who was seeing a movie. She kissed her cheek.

"Grandma, I'm ready to leave. Make sure you take care of yourself".

"My angel, I will and do take care of yourself too.

"Call me", her grandmother said with a sad voice. She hugged her granddaughter.

As they were about to open the door, they heard a knock on the door. Lizzy opened the door. Stan went on his knees immediately the door was opened.

"Lizzy, please come back to me. What you had with my brother was in the past and I still love you", Stan begged.

"I can't be with you and besides I'm traveling to Sweden", she responded.

"Why can't you be with me?" Stan stood up and looked at her for a response.

"I'm still in love with your brother and I don't want to make you feel bad. Let me leave" she looked away from Stan and moved out of the house.

Stan was shocked at her response. She kissed her grandma and gave her a hug.

"Till we meet again Stan. I wish you the best in life." She walked to her taxi and left for the airport, leaving her past behind and moving on to the next chapter of her life.

Printed in the USA
CPSIA information can be obtained
at www.ICGtesting.com
CBHW031133041224
18433CB00027B/332